I0624795

NEW FOUND LOVE

BY

JULIANA BLOSSOM

Copyright

It was about 4:00 one late spring afternoon and I was driving casually up a country road, on the way back to town after doing a soil stability analysis on a rural site. I was coming up on a bicyclist headed the same way, half watching him/her to be sure I wasn't crowding the rider with my F250. The rider was wearing one of those tight, ugly unisex cycling outfits, and I had given up checking out cyclist's rear ends after a couple occasions of discovering, on passing the rider, that the cute butt at one end of the bike had a beard at the front. I've got no problem with gays, but I'm not and I can't help it if I found the experience disturbing. I stuck to watching them just enough to be sure I was sharing the road fairly after that.

I had just swung out to pass the rider with plenty of space when a black and white blur flew out of the roadside bushes and hit the front wheel, sending the rider ass over teakettle. I slammed on the brakes and turned to see a big, ugly dog snapping at the downed rider as he/she tried to fend it off with the bike from a sitting position. Well, that's ridiculous; I grabbed my hawthorn walking stick from behind the seat and jumped out, waving and yelling. The dog turned to me and got a couple good whacks in the ribs before it put its tail between its legs and ran off yelping. I turned to the rider.

"You hurt?"

I looked a little closer. Definitely female, even under the eyesore cycling outfit. She pulled off her helmet, releasing a tangled mass of strawberry blond hair, and looked up at me.

"Scraped up but nothing worse, I think. Where did that thing come from?"

"Must belong to one of those hillbillies out here. Let me help you up."

She started to take my hand and then winced.

"Darn, my hands are really scraped up."

"OK, let's try it this way."

I held her upper arm to keep her steady as she picked herself up. She took a couple steps and then staggered, almost going down, and I threw an arm around her waist. Not a big waist, I noo1ticed in passing. She let me take her light weight.

"You hit your head or something?"

"No, I think it's just adrenaline aftershocks. That was scary."

"No kidding."

I dropped the tailgate and half lifted her onto it.

"Just sit there for a few minutes and get your bearings. Let me see your hands."

She held them out. Both palms were well scraped up, with a couple fairly deep cuts that looked like they had gravel in them. Nice hands otherwise, long fingers well cared for.

"I need the first aid kit. Sit tight a second."

When I came back I noticed a line of blood running down her leg. Potentially attractive legs under better circumstances.

"Looks like your knees took a hit too. How do they feel?"

She swung her legs a little.

"Just scraped and bruised, I think."

She sucked on her lower lip. Cute gesture on her.

"I'm really putting you to a lot of trouble here. Don't you need to go someplace?"

"What am I going to do, leave you ten miles from town injured and with a busted bike? I work for myself so there's no one tracking my time. I'll take off if you insist but I wouldn't feel right about it."

She smiled. A smile that should be registered as a lethal weapon, even through the streaks of mud and sweat across her face.

"I appreciate it, believe me. I just hate to be such a bother."

"Forget it."

I pulled the Leatherman off my belt and folded out the tweezers.

"Let me see those hands again."

I quickly removed the gravel and applied Neosporin and a bandage, and then did the same to her knee.

"You're pretty good at that."

"I was a Devil Doc years ago. Once you've learned to deal with IED injuries a scraped hand is pretty easy. Ready to walk to the door of the truck?"

"You don't have to do all that."

"Like I said, I can't leave you out here stuck. Go hop in."

She carefully walked to the door of the truck, keeping one hand on the side for balance, while I tossed her bike in the back and climbed in the other side.

"First things first. Hi, I'm Ben McLoughlin."

She started to stick out her hand and then thought better of it.

"Jill Williams. I'd normally be glad to meet you, but this way of doing it is painful."

"Hope it doesn't happen often- at least the bike wreck part of it. So, Jill, should I take you home or to the doctor's office?"

"Home would be great. I just want to get cleaned up and get some rest. I live over on Decatur Street."

I tried to make small talk on the way, but she was obviously worn out and struggling to hold up her end, so I let it go and finished the ride in silence except for the directions to her house. She lived in a small house in an older but comfortable part of town, and had a Miata parked in the driveway. She lifted herself out of the truck gingerly, and I climbed out my side.

"Where do you want the bike?"

"Just set it next to the garage for now. Look, you've been really great."

"No problem."

"Well, thanks again."

For the last half of the ride I had been debating whether to suggest that I'd like to see her again. I decided to skip it- she obviously wasn't in any mood to be flirting after the crappy day she'd been having, and it would be sleazy to act like I was expecting something for helping her out.

"Glad to do it. Good luck."

As I drove off I wondered if I was making the biggest mistake of my life.

A couple days later I found an unfamiliar cell phone under the seat of the truck while I was looking for my spare batteries. Nobody on my crew recognized it, but one had the same model and charged it up for me. None of the names in the directory looked familiar, so I took a chance and pushed the "Home" button. I got a female voice.

"Hello?"

"Uh, hello... I'm not sure who I'm calling here but I think I have your cell phone."

Slightly suspicious.

"Who's this?"

"My name's Ben McLoughlin. I found this thing in my truck."

The voice warmed up like the sun popping out from behind a cloud.

"Oh, Ben, this is Jill Williams! Remember you saved me from that dog and gave me a ride home?"

"Of course I remember. You must have dropped your phone. How would you like me to get it back to you?"

"Can we meet up tomorrow?"

"Well, tomorrow's Friday. I have to be out in the field most of the day. How about I buy you a drink after work?"

"Sounds good, but I'm buying. It's the least I can do after you were so helpful."

"You don't owe me anything, but we'll figure something out. Say 6:00 at Anthony's?"

"Works for me. See you then."

Anthony's is a seafood restaurant and bar on the waterfront boardwalk, which makes it a great place to have an after work drink and watch the sunset. I got there early enough to grab a table at the window overlooking the marina and ordered a beer while I waited. As I idly watched a seal in the harbor I heard a low whistle from the next table. I turned and saw most of the men in the bar looking in the same direction. A stunningly beautiful woman in elegant business clothes had just walked in and appeared to be looking around for someone. Some guys have all the luck. Her strawberry blond hair was in a neat French twist- wait, strawberry blonde? I looked again and she saw me, smiled, and strode toward my table, making me the target of all the envious looks for once in my life. I stood up and held her chair.

"Jill? Wow, you clean up well!"

"Thanks. I really wasn't at my best the other day."

"No surprise given the kind of day you were having. How are your hands?"

"No problems, just waiting for them to heal."

She showed me her palms, which did look better. Graceful gold watch, no hint of a ring- this was looking better all the time.

"What did you say you were? A Devil Dog?"

"No, a Devil Dog is a Marine. I was a Devil Doc- a Navy corpsman attached to a Marine unit. That was a long time ago, though."

"Sounds scary."

"Not really. I got out years back. Actually, I spent most of my service in Korea. Sometimes I thought that every new Marine had to learn the hard way not to fight with Korean civilians. I patched up more drunk jarheads on Saturday nights than I care to remember."

There actually had been some pretty scary nights along the DMZ, but why bring up a downer like that?

"You in medicine now?"

"No, I'm a civil engineer. The Navy was more a growing up experience than a career choice. So what do you do?"

"I'm a lawyer with the state Department of Justice."

"How did you get into that?"

The waitress came by and Jill ordered a glass of Chardonnay for herself and another Red Hook for me. The conversation never slowed down, and before we knew it the sun was all the way down.

"Want to order some dinner? Any other plans tonight?"

"Dinner sounds great. All I was going to do tonight was read a bunch of work files."

"Sad thing for a pretty woman to be doing on a Friday night."

She shrugged.

"Thanks. I'm too busy for much of a social life outside of work and I learned the hard way that dating other lawyers is a dead end street. The legal community gossips more than my college sorority. This is the closest I've come to a date in months."

"So is this a date or a friendly dinner?"

She winked.

"Depends. Are you going to try to kiss me goodnight?"

"Should I?"

She rolled her dark blue eyes.

"Never ask a woman's permission to kiss her. Just try it if it feels right and see what happens."

"So we'll know if this is a date or not at the end of the evening?"

Her eyes twinkled.

"I guess you'll have to try it and see what happens."

Dinner was good, although I don't remember a bit of what we ate. I was too busy talking with Jill about anything and everything to notice.

"You always carry a big stick in your truck?"

"I got out of the military partly because of a knee injury. It usually doesn't bother me but sometimes I have to cover some rough ground for my job, and it helps. Not to mention it's useful for some other things, as you saw."

"Any good stories out of the injury?"

"It was just a dumb accident. They didn't even give me a Purple Heart for it."

"What happened?"

"The unit was taking our turn patrolling the DMZ. One night some dumbass lit a smoke in the open, and of course some North Korean took a potshot at the light. The guy started screaming for a corpsman, and I came running and stepped in a hole. Turned out later the round bounced off his helmet and didn't even draw blood, but the way he was screaming we thought he was dying. I was the only one actually injured."

Jill shook her head.

"What happened to him?"

"The gunny told him that he was too stupid to be out on patrol and made him the permanent shit burner- excuse me, latrine orderly- for the rest of the rotation. It was summer and he was a lot smarter by the time we rotated back to Seoul. Look, when I start talking about the service I unconsciously start talking like we did back then. Sorry."

"Nothing I haven't heard before. Don't worry about it."

About the third time the waiter asked if we wanted anything else the hint sank in.

"I think they want this table back. Want to go for a walk on the boardwalk?"

"Sure. Let me go grab my coat."

I settled the bill and met her at the front door and we strolled out toward the point. About the third time our hands bumped our fingers got entwined and stayed that way. This was going better than I would have thought possible. Jill was smart and enthusiastic about life, making her a real kick to hang out with ⍰uite aside from her remarkable looks. No idea what she wanted with an average guy like me, but she seemed to be having as good a time as I was.

We paused at the end of the boardwalk, looking back at the lights of town.

"Kind of windy out here, isn't it?"

Jill shivered slightly and moved in front of me out of the wind, leaning back a little against my chest. I wrapped my arms lightly around her slim shoulders and looked down to find her looking back and up at me with her eyebrows raised in a slightly challenging expression. I remembered something one of my professors used to say about "a tide in the affairs of men, which, when taken at the flood..." Oh, the hell with that; I leaned down and captured her lips gently. She didn't resist, thank God. In fact, I felt a slight smile as the initial wind chill faded against my mouth. She rotated in my arms enough to reach up and run one hand through the hair behind my ear, cupping the back of my head slightly. The spicy, flowery scent of her perfume was faint but still nearly knocked me out. I kept it light; she wasn't the type to appreciate being groped and mauled in public. By the time we broke, though, it was clear that she had absolutely no problem with a public kiss. She still had a smile on her face.

"That was nice."

"You're the master- or maybe the mistress- of understatement. I'm not sure I can feel my legs. I guess this is officially a date?"

"Well, to make it official, you're going to have to walk me to my car and see what happens when we say goodnight. This has been a lot of fun, but it's really late and I do have some things to do tomorrow."

I checked my watch.

"My God, I never realized it was this late. That car of yours doesn't turn into a pumpkin, does it?"

"Not in the five years of so I've had it. First time for everything, though."

We turned back toward town and her hand naturally fell into mine. Neither of us was in any great hurry to get back to her car. I knew the evening was going to end there, which didn't bother me, but I was really enjoying her company. Eventually we got to the parking lot. She unlocked her car, opened the door, and looked up at me.

"Well..."

She glanced around at the empty lot.

"Don't ask, Ben, just try it and see what happens..."

I slid my arms around her waist, and her arms locked around my neck. This was a far deeper, more passionate kiss than the first time, and our hands were starting to wander by the time she pulled back. She smiled at me.

"I think that officially makes this our first date. You wrote down my phone number before you gave that cell phone back, right?"

"Give me credit for some intelligence. Of course I did."

"Good. Call me and we'll make plans to do this again."

"I can't wait."

"Neither can I. Good night."

With a 𝕢uick final kiss she was gone.

It took me a few seconds to figure out why I woke up smiling Saturday morning. Then I spent the next half hour or so reliving the previous evening in glorious detail before I got up and started my regular Saturday bachelor chores. It seemed hard to believe that such a beautiful, classy woman would be interested in an average guy like me, but her actions spoke louder than words.

I waited until Sunday afternoon to call her, and she sounded happy to hear from me.

"Ben! What's up?"

"I was just thinking about you and wanted to see how you're doing. I also wanted to say thanks for going out with me the other night. I haven't had that much fun in a long time."

"I had a lot of fun too."

Next step was obvious, and I had to take it.

"You said something about doing it again."

"I'd like that."

"You like sailing? I have a sailboat, and I was thinking we could take it out next weekend. Maybe run out to Johnson Island, have lunch, and bring it back."

"I've never done much sailing but I'd like to learn. Saturday?"

"Saturday would be good. Let's plan on it."

We agreed to talk later about specifics, chatted a while, and rang off. When I looked at the clock I realized that we had been on the phone for a solid two hours. That girl was so easy to talk with that I constantly lost track of time. Strange feeling, but I enjoyed it.

The next week was a busy one. An old college friend was now a lawyer in town, and he was involved in a lawsuit over the failure of an old earthen dam back in the hills. A couple of farms had been flooded out, and now the lawyers were arguing over who was going to pay for the damage. Ed had called me for help understanding the failure analysis reports. Before I knew it, I was listed as an expert witness and had to sit for a deposition. I met Ed the day before to get ready.

"Remember, you're the guy in the room who understands the science here. Be ready to justify your conclusions, but don't go beyond what the data and analysis will support. Whatever you do, don't let them make you mad."

"I'll be fine, Ed. What are a bunch of lawyers going to come up with that's worse than what I dealt with in the service?"

I was thrown for a loop, though, when I walked in and saw a familiar head of strawberry blonde hair on the other side of the table. Ed did the introductions.

"Angus McLoughlin, this is Jill Williams, the attorney for the State Water Division."

Jill stood up and extended a hand.

"Glad to meet you, Angus."

She had a strange look in her eyes, and I quickly decided to follow her lead and not expose her private life in front of all these other people. We sat down and got started.

Some lawyers try to intimidate witnesses with word games and snotty attitudes, but the better ones make sure they know their stuff ahead of time. Jill was one of the good ones; she hit every point where there was room for a difference of opinion and made me acknowledge it, while I explained why

I thought my opinion the stronger one. It turned into almost an academic discussion instead of a cross examination. She had obviously been studying the engineering issues thoroughly, and by the end I was about ready to offer her a job as a trainee if she got tired of practicing law. Once we got through the facts she started the personal questions.

"How much of your work is as an expert witness?"

"This is the first time I've done it. Ed's an old friend and asked for help."

"What are you charging for your time?"

"Nothing. I got involved as a favor to Ed, as I said, and wasn't expecting it to go this far."

"So you're working for free?"

"Ed's clients are decent folks who didn't deserve to get their farm and livelihood wiped out because someone else was careless. I don't need to make money off them."

I looked at Ed and shrugged.

"For the record, though, Ed owes me a bottle of Laphroaigh when this is all over."

"Of what?"

"It's a single malt whisky from the part of Scotland my grandfather came from."

"You're doing all this work for a bottle of whisky?"

I shrugged.

"I think you lawyers call it pro bono. The Scotch is just a guy thing."

She looked surprised, and possibly impressed, and Quickly wrapped up. When it was done Ed and I went back to his office to debrief.

"So what was that odd look you and Ms. Williams gave each other at the start?"

I sighed. He didn't get where he is by missing much.

"I had dinner with her Friday night."

His jaw dropped.

"Dinner as in a date?"

"Well, yeah. It didn't start out that way but that's how it ended up."

Ed banged his forehead on the desk a couple times.

"I don't know whether to be outraged that opposing counsel would date my expert witness or impressed that you got that iceberg to go out with you."

"Iceberg? She's the warmest woman I've met in years! And just for the record, the case never came up once. I don't think she realized I was involved until we walked in this morning."

"I have to believe that. She's tough, but she's never been less than totally honest. She's not the type to play around with my witnesses behind my back. You know how many men have tried to flirt or get a date with her and run into a brick wall? She's beautiful, but she keeps every man I know at arm's length."

"She did say something about how getting involved with other lawyers is nothing but trouble professionally."

He glanced at his computer monitor.

"Here's the e-mail already. Hmm... Letting me know that she had dinner with you, purely social, the case never came up, and of course it's not going to happen again while this case is going on. Sorry, man, I guess you're not going to be seeing the bar's hottest pair of legs outside of court until this is over." He paused.

"Come to think of it she was wearing pants today, wasn't she? Well, her rear end in a pair of slacks is pretty stunning too."

"Keep it up, you lecher, and I'm telling Kim!"

Ed glanced up.

"Wow, you must really like her. You know I like looking at women, and you've never threatened to tell Kim before."

"Tell me what?"

Ed's wife had walked in without my hearing her. Kim's small, delicately pretty, and runs her family with an iron hand in a velvet glove.

"That you're way too good for him. When are you going to dump this joker and run off to Tahiti with me?"

I made a halfhearted grab at her just to give her an excuse to squeal and jump into Ed's lap. She giggled as she cuddled up to him.

"When elephants fly, jerk! You've been giving me that line since before our wedding, and I keep telling you the same thing. I'd rather have my man who knows he's lucky to have me than a smartass with delusions of superiority."

She waved the big rock on her left hand at me.

"Go find your own woman, Ben. This one is all Ed's and that's how I like it!"

Ed kissed her, laughing. It was true that we'd been kidding around like this since we had all met in college. Those two were so devoted to each other that no one took it as anything but a joke.

"He's finally working on it. He was just telling me about his date with Jill Williams last weekend."

Kim's eyes widened.

"That blonde who almost caused a riot when she walked into the Bar Association Christmas party in a little cocktail dress? And you call Ed outclassed! How did you manage that?"

"Literally by accident."

I told them the story about the bike wreck. Kim shook her head when we got to the part about how Jill wasn't going to see me outside of court while the case was open.

"Well, Ed, you better get it resolved quickly before this poor schnook loses the plot. He's obviously got it bad. Couldn't find a more elegant woman to fall for, though. Now come on, I came down here so you guys could take me to lunch."

Jill called me that evening.

"Well, that was a shock seeing you this morning. What's this 'Angus B. McLoughlin' stuff? I never made the connection."

"Old family tradition, but if you had a first name like 'Angus' you might go by your middle name too. You can imagine what they called me in junior high."

"I can see that. Look, I can't tell you how much I regret this, but there's no way I can go out with you while this case is going on."

I sighed.

"Yeah, Ed told me about the e-mail. No way around this, is there?"

"I wouldn't take it if there was. There are lines I can't cross professionally, and you're on the wrong side of one of them. Once this case is over with, though, I hope we can pick up where we left off."

"I hope so too. I'll keep the first mate slot open."

"First mate already?"

"Would you prefer galley wench? I need one of those too."

She laughed.

"First mate it is. I really am sorry about this, Ben."

"So am I. Talk to you later."

Ed called me two months later.

"Hey, Angus, your dream girl got the State's side of the case dismissed. She's not off limits any more, so you can stop finding excuses to ask me twice a week."

"Don't call me Angus, jerk, and don't poke fun at Jill. Thanks for letting me know, though."

"Still sensitive about her, eh? Well, enjoy it. She's a nice gal and a hell of a lawyer."

Jill called me after work. She sounded nervous.

Ben? It's Jill Williams. Remember me? I resolved that case, so if you want to get together sometime, it's not a problem..."

"Hey, that's great! Want to go sailing this weekend?"

"Love to. Listen, you doing anything tonight?"

"Nothing important. Why?"

"Some of my coworkers dragged me out to a bar to celebrate winning the case and it's getting old fast. If you want to come pick me up we could hang out a while."

"I'll be there in fifteen minutes."

When I got to the bar Jill hugged me, kissed me on the cheek, and dragged me around with her hand firmly in mine to introduce me to a few people before announcing that she was leaving with me. It seemed a little over the top, but why should I complain about her being happy to see me? When we got in the truck it made more sense.

"I hope I wasn't coming on too strong. Some of those dorks get a couple of drinks in them and think they're God's gift to women. Being seen leaving early with a good looking guy is going to save me stress later. I hope you don't mind."

"Having a pretty woman pretending I'm her boyfriend? It's a tough job, but if it's for a good cause, I guess I can tolerate it. Any side benefits?"

She punched me in the arm.

"Keep hoping! Are you always this full of it?"

"Most of the time. You want to go get dinner?"

"It's been a long few days getting this case settled, and I have to go to work tomorrow. Would it be OK if we just got some takeout and went to my place? I'm too tired for anything fancy."

"Fine with me. Szechuan Heaven?"

"Sounds good."

Her house was simple and neat on the inside with lots of interesting photography she'd done. She pointed me to the kitchen.

"Would you mind getting out the plates while I change out of my work clothes? There's some Tsingtao in the refrigerator if you want it."

"Should I get you something to drink?"

"Just a soda, thanks."

She came back in tennis shorts and a t-shirt that left just a little strip of skin showing above the waistband. Simple, comfortable, sexy- was there anything this girl didn't do well? I could well believe that she had the best legs in the Bar, too. We got into a casual chopstick duel over the last kung pao shrimp, which I promptly fed to her when I won. The smile in her eyes made it more than worth it. She stretched.

"Let's leave this mess for later and go catch the late news. I want to see if they said anything about my case."

I flopped on her couch, she flopped right next to me and put her feet up on the coffee table so I did too. She put both hands around my bicep and laid her head on my shoulder, and we played a little casual footsie while we watched the news. As it ended I glanced at her.

"Looks like they missed it... Jill?"

It takes a heck of a woman to look cute when she's snoring, but she did it. Time to call it a night; I gently disentangled myself, got her all the way on the couch, covered her with the blanket that was draped over the back, and kissed her cheek. Her eyes fluttered.

"Ben?"

"I'm calling it a night, sweetheart. I'll call you later about the weekend."

I don't think she was all the way awake.

"You're a great guy, Ben. Good night."

Not exactly the way I had hoped the night would end, but I could live with it.

Saturday morning she came skipping down the dock bright and early with a smile on her face.

"Morning, Ben! Nice boat!"

"Thanks. I built most of it myself. Jump aboard."

She handed me her backpack and then took my hand and stepped aboard. I took the chance to snatch a quick kiss, and she responded enthusiastically.

"Sorry I was such a bad hostess the other night."

"Forget it. Take a look around below if you want. I'm going to get the sail set and get us out of the marina."

She disappeared for a few seconds and then came back on deck.

"Nice setup here. Can I help?"

"Sure, grab that line there and pull until I tell you to stop."

She obviously didn't know much about sailing but was more than willing to take directions. I tacked a couple times and got us settled on a long reach out toward the island. Jill dropped below and came back with a couple of cups, handing me one.

"I figured out the stove. Hope the coffee's how you like it."

I took a sip.

"OK, you're officially the galley wench."

"Galley wench? What happened to first mate?"

"No reason you can't be both."

She settled herself beside me in the cockpit, and we drank our coffee in a companionable silence.

"What's that smile?"

"I was just thinking. Beautiful day, enough wind, and a gorgeous woman beside me in my boat. Sailing doesn't get much better than this."

Jill studied her cup thoughtfully.

"Ben, I want to be honest with you, and I don't know if I can say this without sounding like a stuck up bitch."

"You've never been less than honest before, and you're about as far from the other as you could get. Go ahead."

"People have been telling me how good looking I am as long as I can remember, and it's never made a lot of sense. I don't think I'm all that pretty, but other people seem to and maybe they're right. It's nothing I did, though. I try to take care of myself and stay in shape, but the rest of it is just genetics. Why compliment me if I got lucky with my ancestors?"

"Well, I think you're about the most beautiful woman I've ever met, but if you don't want me saying so I'll stop."

"You're different. There's something to be said for attracting handsome single men."

She thought a second.

"I worked hard in law school, and I work hard as a lawyer. If someone wants to be impressed by my legal work that's great. Being attractive just seems to make it that much harder to be taken seriously as a lawyer. I may kill the next person who tells me that a girl as pretty as I am doesn't need to work for a living. The girls I knew in college that went that route are either married to older men and bored out of their minds or desperate to get married before they get any older. I think I'm actually pretty good at law, and I want people I deal with to judge me by my work, not my looks. It's one reason I had to put you off limits for so long. People would have thought I was dating you to get an edge on the case."

"From what I saw the other day you are pretty damn good at law. I know Ed thinks so too, although just between you and me he's also made a couple comments about how I'm dating the hottest woman in the Bar Association."

She laughed.

"Ed's all bark and no bite. He tries to hide how devoted he is to his family. I can't be offended by that. The fact that he thinks so much of you was a definite point in your favor. So you don't think I'm a stuck up bitch?"

"I think you're a sweet, smart, talented woman. Is it OK if I think you're hot too?"

She grinned and kissed me on the cheek.

"You, sir, are welcome to think anything you want."

It was getting hot by the time we headed back after lunch. I went below for a soda and almost dropped it when I came back up and saw Jill's shorts and sweatshirt in a pile on the bow, next to her stretched out body.

"If you don't want men noticing your looks, that bikini is a step in the wrong direction."

She sat up and looked around.

"How many men are in sight?"

"Well, just me, I guess."

"Figure it out, genius. You need any help with the boat?"

"Not really."

"I'm going to work on my tan for a while, then. Actually, this bikini belongs to my girlfriend. She said that if a hot guy was taking me sailing my old Speedo wasn't good enough."

She looked down at herself and grimaced.

"I forgot that she's a half size smaller than I am."

"I don't see the problem."

"You wouldn't, would you? Typical man."

"Thank her for me the next time you see her, OK?"

She laughed and laid back down. My mind was racing ahead to the marina. Sailing in with what looked like a stray from a Sports Illustrated swimsuit shoot on the bow would get me enthusiastic service from the teenage dock boys for a long time to come. I wandered back to check the tiller and GPS for the point where I wanted to tack to get to the marina in one reach.

As we got there I went to swing the boom and made the mistake of glancing at Jill, now dozing on her flat belly on the bow. She had untied the top of her bikini and moved the strings off to the side. Sensible move if a girl wants to avoid tan lines, but a lot to spring on a guy without warning. Definitely distracted me at the wrong time. As the boat came around the boom swung across and caught me in the stomach, and I instinctively grabbed it as it carried me over the rail. The sudden tilt of the boat and my frenzied cursing brought Jill leaping to her feet.

"What are you doing?"

"Grab that line and pull me back in! Quick!"

She did so and then doubled up laughing.

"Oh, Ben, if you could have seen the look on your face!"

"Whacked in the ribs, hanging out there over the water, and being rescued by a topless first mate doesn't happen every day."

"Top...?"

She glanced down.

"Oh Lord!"

She crossed her arms, blushing furiously, and then took a deep breath and looked around.

"Oh, hell, no one out here but us and you've gotten a good look already."

She casually picked up her tank top and pulled it on, with a little extra bounce for my benefit. My turn to laugh.

"Talk about surprised looks! You should have seen the look on your face. Your breasts are a lovely work of art, by the way."

She blushed and grinned at the same time.

"No they're not. One hundred percent natural, and I don't appreciate you suggesting otherwise."

"That's not what I- ah, hell, you know what I mean."

She laughed at my confusion, I laughed at her, and before we knew it we were both laughing helplessly. She collapsed into my arms and I took a step back and sat heavily on top of the deckhouse, cradling her slender body. It took a while but eventually the laughter slowed down and we regained control. Then she looked at me and it started again. Finally she pulled herself up and wiped her eyes.

"I haven't laughed that hard in I don't know how long."

She glanced over my shoulder.

"Uh, Ben, are we supposed to be this close to shore?"

I spun around. Not being under proper control, the boat had drifted into a deserted cove and was getting too close to the beach for comfort.

"Oh, crap!"

I ran forward and dropped the anchor to give myself time to sort out the situation. Once I stopped the drift I took a look at the wind.

"We're going to be stuck here a while. I can't sail out of this cove with the wind in this direction. There's usually an offshore breeze that comes up around sunset, and once it does we'll be in good shape to get back."

Jill shrugged.

"I wasn't in any rush to go anywhere. Come give me a hand in the galley."

I set up the table in the cockpit and took the tray of cheese and crackers she handed me. Then she handed me a bottle of Roederer.

"Can you open that?"

"Sure. Where did this come from?"

"Gift for winning that case. I meant to share it with you Wednesday night, but I was so tired I forgot and fell asleep."

I popped the cork and poured us each a glass.

"Here's tae us, wha's like us?"

"Damn few, and they're all dead."

She grinned again at the look on my face.

"You aren't the only one on this boat who had a Scottish grandfather."

"I guess not."

We fell silent for a while, sipping champagne and watching the sun set.

"Penny for your thoughts?"

"You're an amazing woman. Educated, smart, sophisticated, and incredibly pretty whether you like it or not. What do you want with an average guy like me?"

Jill sighed, put down her glass, and sat in my lap, resting her arms casually around my shoulders.

"In the first place you aren't an average guy. Ask any of my girlfriends if it's easy to find a sane, intelligent, responsible single man these days. Men like you are rarer than you think. I also see a man who habitually does the right thing without worrying about himself, which is pretty cool. Being good with your hands is sexy. Last but not least, I think you're pretty good looking yourself. I like you a lot and I get the impression you like me too."

"I have the world's biggest crush on you, and you know it."

She shifted to straddle me on the cockpit bench, giving me a very female smile.

"I suspected, anyway. Don't over think this, Ben. Stop putting me on a pedestal and telling yourself I'm some sort of goddess. I'm just an ordinary girl who's learned to put up a good front, and I'm definitely not more than you deserve. Let's enjoy this and see where it goes."

"This?"

Her lips came within a half inch of mine, and she whispered.

"This."

I pulled her the rest of the way into a long, deep kiss. As it continued my lips drifted down her neck to her collarbone, and farther still to those glorious breasts she was pressing into my face. The soft cotton of her tank top kept getting in my way, so I pulled it over her head with her willing help. Her skin tasted of salt spray and coconut oil, and under it a warm smell of happy, excited woman. She shuddered as her small puffy nipples disappeared into my mouth, first one and then the other.

"Oh my God, that feels so good. Don't stop..."

Stopping was the last thing I wanted to do. My hands slid down her back and found the bow ties at her hips that held her bikini bottom on. One good pull and I tossed it aside.

"You OK with this?"

"Have I told you to stop?"

I kissed her again and reached down under her spread hips to her hot, wet center, running my fingers along and then between her moist lower lips. She gasped and tightened her grip on my shoulders further. Then she sat back and attacked my belt and shorts, loosening them as fast as she could. I arched under her a little and I was naked too. She put her arms around my neck and looked down at me, pushing my face into her cleavage.

"Oh, this is incredible.."

I entered her slightly. She paused a couple of seconds and then slid down the rest of the way, wiggling a little to get me as deep as possible. She was hot and wet and tight, and it felt so good I would willingly have held her like that all night. After a couple minutes she started rocking slightly, and that felt even better. I wrapped my arms around her and helped her slide up and down, all the way in and out. I got a nipple in my mouth again. She was half moaning a steady stream of comments:

"Oh, that's nice...so nice... just like that...this is good, so good... oh yes...yes... oh my GOD!" I felt the waves of orgasm start from deep inside her and engulf her whole body, and that was all it took to push me over the edge. She sagged onto my shoulder, suddenly boneless, and I held her tight while caressing her back. I felt a wetness on my shoulder and heard what sounded like a quiet sob.

"Jill? My God, did I hurt you?"

I started to lift her off me, but her arms and legs tightened.

"No, but if you pull out now I may hurt you."

She lifted her head and kissed me, and I would swear she came again.

"Of course you didn't hurt me, silly. Couldn't you tell that I was enjoying that as much as you were? I just had the most overwhelming sexual experience of my life with what may be the best man I've ever known, and I'm crying because I'm happy. I know it's silly and girly and illogical and all those other things I try not to be, but right now I don't give a damn."

"Jill, I know you're a hell of a lawyer, but good lawyers aren't hard to find. A man only finds a woman like you once in a lifetime, and that's if he's lucky. I want you as a woman, and you can be as silly and girly as you want."

I know that technically a man can't be held responsible for anything he says while he has a naked girl wrapped around him, but what was happening that night was so mind blowing that I couldn't think of anything to say but the truth.

"God, if those people I scare in court could see me now..."

"Naked and in a post-orgasmic daze? I think I'll save that privilege for myself, although I intend to get you into this condition fre�uently."

"Promise?"

I kissed her.

"Promise."

Eventually I popped out of her, and she picked herself up and pulled her tank top back on. We were both staggering a little, and not because the boat was moving.

"You have any big plans tomorrow?"

"Not really. Why?"

"I'd rather not sail back in the pitch dark if we don't need to. Why don't we spend the night here and head back in the morning?" "Well, that's a pretty small bunk below. Might be a tight fit for two, but as long as it's for a good cause, I'm willing."

She was actually more than willing. The solution we found was to spend most of the night swapping places on top of each other, with occasional variations and naps. I woke up with that glorious bare body sprawled across me and strawberry blond hair tickling my nose. After laying there thinking and feeling for a few minutes, I ran my free hand over the long, smooth curves of her back, hip and thigh a few times. She stirred and looked up at me, smiling.

"Good morning, handsome."

"Morning, beautiful."

"You make a lumpy mattress."

"Well, you make a lumpy blanket."

My hand captured one of her more interesting lumps.

"Not that I'm complaining."

"I should hope not."

By this time my thumb was rolling her right nipple in lazy circles.

"This is a very nice lump."

"Is it just me, or are you getting lumpier by the minute?"

"Not just you. Something about pretty naked girls gets me all lumpy."

"I think I can fix that."

Her legs gripped my hips, and I slid into her. She started to sit up, but I grabbed her around the ribs.

"Careful there, sweetheart. Mind the overhead."

"I... oh yes... forgot that...no matter...this is really good..."

She was slowly rocking back and forth, rubbing those lovely breasts up and down my chest. She kissed me.

"This is... oh yeah... a great way to...wake up..."

No argument there. It went on for a long time, the tension slowly building. I pulled her back into a kiss. She whispered.

"Oh,... this is so damn...NICE!"

As she spilled over the edge I went with her, almost passing out from the intensity of the moment. She rested lazily on top of me for a while before she stirred.

"Time to head back?"

"Yeah, I think so."

"I'll make the coffee while you set the sails."

"Deal."

On the way to the bow a flame in the galley caught the corner of my eye. I spun and looked closer- a fire on a boat is no joke- to find Jill, casually naked, reaching into an overhead locker with a beam of sunshine lighting up the small reddish yellow triangle at the junction of her thighs. It was a sight I hoped I would remember on my deathbed. She looked over, caught me gawking, and gave me a knowing grin and a thumb pointing toward the bow. I pulled my thoughts back to business and got the boat moving.

Back at the dock, she helped tie up the boat and clean up, and I walked her up to her Miata.

"Want to come by my place for a while?"

"I hate to say this, but I have things I have to get done before Monday. Why don't you call me in a day or two?"

"OK. Thanks for coming out with me."

"The pleasure was all mine."

"Not hardly, but it sure was fun."

"Yeah, it was."

She kissed me and drove off, and I couldn't stop grinning all the way home.

I couldn't wait any longer than Monday night to call her up.

"How was work today?"

"Same old, same old. On to the next case, but at least they're giving me the bigger stuff now. How about you?"

"I'm getting all sorts of calls from lawyers who need an engineering expert. I guess the word is that I did a good job on that last case."

"You did do a good job. Your analysis was convincing, you backed it up thoroughly, and Ed's clients got paid off quickly by the company that actually did the damage. Are you going to take the work?"

"I think so. The money's good and the work is interesting."

"I'm going to put you on the list as someone we should use. You're impressive when you want to be. Speaking of which, when are we getting together again?"

"Want to come over for dinner tomorrow?"

"Sure."

My house was originally a weekend beach cabin, and was built partially on pilings over the bay. No way it would be allowed today, but it's grandfathered in. The view from the deck just above the water is pretty incredible. I hit the grocery store and the oyster farm up the road early, and had dinner well under way when Jill's Miata eased its way down the access road to my tiny waterfront yard. I met her at the door.

"Neat place you have here."

"It's not big, but I like it. Come on in."

As soon as the door closed behind her she wrapped her arms around my neck and kissed me hungrily. I responded enthusiastically, and before I knew it she was unbuttoning my shirt and loosening my belt. I managed to get her skirt off before she shoved me down on the floor, pulled her hot pink lace thong aside, and mounted me. When I got her blouse unbuttoned I found a bra that matched the thong and seemed designed for easy removal. Once I had her naked I grabbed her and rolled her onto her back, breaking just long enough to pull the thong off. She had her legs wrapped around me and was moving in rhythm, faster and faster until she reached a screaming orgasm that took me right along with it. I looked down at her, kissed her again, and rolled off, holding her hand.

"That's a hell of a way to say hello, honey."

"I spent the whole day deep in thought on a brief I'm writing, and really needed to do something physical. I was going to suggest we go for a walk, but then I saw you and suddenly had a better idea. I hope you don't mind."

"Mind? Mind being half raped by my beautiful girl? Are you kidding? I hope they put you on appeals full time!"

"Don't even think that. So I'm your girl?"

"I want you to be, but don't let me rush you."

"I like the idea too."

She pulled herself up for a long deep kiss, and we left it at that for the time being.

"What's that smell?"

"I better go check dinner."

I picked myself up and then helped her up.

"I can't face getting back into my work clothes."

"You look fine to me now."

"Yeah, right! I'm not eating dinner in the nude. Can I raid your closet?"

"Sure, help yourself. Right through that door."

I went to check dinner while she disappeared and came back wearing an old "EDDIE WOULD GO" T-shirt and not much else. She came over and sniffed at the stove, and I took the chance to snatch a kiss. My hand ended up on her trim rear end.

"Pretty wild lingerie for a serious lawyer."

"I may have to dress in serious, somber suits, but I can still be a girl underneath."

"So every time I unwrap you it's a surprise?"

"Something like that."

She glanced down.

"Who's Eddie, anyway?"

"Eddie Aikau. Great Hawaiian surfer and lifeguard who was legendary for surfing the big waves that everyone else was scared to try."

"Cool. You surf?"

"Not seriously. I picked up the shirt on vacation. Here, try these oysters."

We ate dinner and finished our wine on the deck.

"Want to spend the night?"

"Want to, yes, but I don't have a change of clothes for work tomorrow with me."

"I'll make some room for you in my closet."

"Good plan."

She ran a finger down my chest.

"I'm thinking about taking advantage of you again before I go."

"I guess what they say about oysters is true. How about I take advantage of you?"

"That works too."

So I carried her into the bedroom and took thorough advantage of her before she borrowed some sweats, walked a little gingerly to her car, and went home.

Before long, we were getting into the habit of spending about half our nights together at one house or the other. It was a comfortable situation for both of us: we knew we were crazy about each other and would rather be together than apart, but didn't get upset if the other was busy with something else. Most weekends we spent sailing, backpacking, or traveling around the Northwest. Her first evening at my house wasn't a fluke, either. After a long day of intellectual hard work, she tended to come home ready to get seriously physical. I felt like I had hit the jackpot, as if I didn't think that already. I asked her about it late one night after she was worn out and cuddled up to me ready to go to sleep.

"So what did you do with all this excess energy before you met me?"

"Lots of running and biking. I'm going to have to watch my figure now that I'm spending so much time in bed."

"I've been watching your figure, believe me, and it's perfect. Any time you need more exercise, though, just let me know."

"You sure talk a good game. Sounds good, actually, but we need to get some sleep. Tomorrow's a work day."

One day I got a call from Kim.

"Rumor is that you and Jill Williams have been seeing a lot of each other."

"Really? People must have a lot of time on their hands to be keeping track of my love life."

"Nice try, Ben. You know I spend most of my time chasing our twins these days. I need my fix of romance somewhere."

"How are my two favorite three year olds?"

"The boys are great. Hyperactive as always. If you carve them any more whistles, though, Jill may see those pictures from junior year spring break."

"What good is the train set I made them without sound effects?"

"Just wait until you have kids! Anyway, when are you going to bring her over for dinner?"

"When are you inviting us? Is it OK with Ed?"

"Ed likes her a lot. So do I, for that matter. How about Saturday?"

"Works for me. Let me check with Jill and get back to you."

The twins seemed to like the two wooden dump trucks I had made for them even without sound effects. I noticed that they were careful to say 'thank you" under Kim's watchful eye before scampering off to play with them. Jill and Ed had that odd lawyer thing going where they can beat each other's brains out all day and then be friends as soon as the whistle blows. Good friends, good food, and some good wine made for a really great evening.

Kim called me a couple days later.

"So, dummy, you think you're ever going to find a better woman than Jill?"

"I don't think one exists except for you, and I'm tired of trying to steal you from Ed."

"Glad to hear that, since it's never going to happen. Seriously, though, why haven't you closed the deal yet? The only thing wrong with Jill is that she was dumb enough to fall head over heels for you. If you're smart you'll marry her before she wises up."

"Marry her? Jesus, I never thought that far ahead. Dating her is too much fun. Why mess with a good thing?"

A sudden, unworthy thought struck me.

"Wait, did she put you up to this?"

"Hell, no, and if she finds out I'm going to lose my new tennis partner. Do you really think that girl's afraid to speak her mind about anything?"

"You're right. She's better than that and so are you."

"Damn straight. Think about it, though. Most women expect a relationship to move forward. She may not buy into the 'why mess with a good thing' theory forever. Don't screw this up, Ben. She's good people and so are you, although I'll deny I ever said that."

Kim might be a little—or sometimes a lot—bossy, but she was a very smart woman underneath it and I knew she cared about me. She had chewed me out before for fooling around with airheads, so having her tell me to hurry up and marry a girl was new. Things fell apart before I really got my head around the idea.

"Angus, you jerk, why would you take a case where I'm on the other side?"

Jill calling me 'Angus' was not a good sign.

"I don't take cases against the State. What's going on?"

I just got the witness list on the S◻ualichuk Landslide trial, and you're on it!"

I thought back over it.

"They told me they were on the same side as the State when they asked me to do that job."

"Well, there's five sides to that thing, and positions shift a lot. You're against us now, and I can't see you outside of court until it's over. You know the rules. Damn it, this was bad enough the first time, and that was before we, well, you know."

"I know. Have I mentioned how much I enjoyed the 'you know' in the shower this morning?"

"Not on a work line, Ben! This is serious."

She whispered.

"If this doesn't get sorted out you're going to be showering alone for a long time. I can't even ask you to back out."

"Maybe you can't, but you can't tell me not to either. I need to call my employers on this thing."

I called the lawyer who had hired me.

"That thing with the State only happened this morning. How did you find out about it so fast?"

"Jill Williams called me."

"Why the heck is she calling you? That's out of line!"

"Look, she's your opposing counsel, but she's my girlfriend."

"Really? Wow, you're a lucky man."

"I know it, and that's why I told you up front I wouldn't take a case against the State. This puts her in a really bad spot."

"I see the problem, and I take back the comment about her being out of line. She's not like that. Even so, I can't just let you out of it."

"Look, I'll give your money back if that's the problem."

"It's not. You've already done the work and I don't have time to find another expert before the trial. The deadline's passed already. Without you I don't have a case."

"And if I stay in it my girlfriend's off limits until the trial. Crap. Look, I need to talk to her about what happens next. What if we promise not to talk about the case?"

"I would actually trust both of you on that, but let me talk to the client."

"I need to at least tell Jill I'm working on it."

"Of course. If I was dating her I'd walk across molten lava barefoot not to blow it."

I let that one go; while I felt the same way it wasn't his place to comment on it.

Jill wasn't having it, unfortunately.

"What happens if I beat you up on cross examination and then it comes out that I'm sleeping with you? I can't afford to look ridiculous in trial. If you can't get out of it we're going to have to take a break. You know it's not what I want, but I don't see anything else we can do."

"Damn it, Jill...,"

"Don't get mad at me, Ben. This wasn't my mistake. You know how much you mean to me, and I'm sure as heck not trying to break up with you."

"I know, Jill. I feel the same way about you. I just hate the idea that I'm screwing things up with some dumb mistake."

"It's only a few weeks. I know you're kind of dense, but I'm trying to tell you that you haven't screwed anything up long term. We'll be fine when this is over."

"Good. Don't make any plans for the weekend after the trial."

"I won't. Talk to you later."

It was unbelievable how much not seeing Jill sucked. It wasn't only the terrific sex I missed, although that was bad enough. I kept catching myself looking forward to seeing her at the end of the day or asking her what she thought about something, and then realizing with a fresh pain that I wasn't going to be able to. She had really gotten under my skin. I had built what I thought was a healthy, satisfying life as a single man, and now none of it meant anything without her. Kim, of course, knew what ailed me.

"Ben, you dope, your secretary called me asking if we were hiring at the law firm. She says there's no living with you these days. How long has she been with you?"

"Close to five years. Why didn't she talk to me?"

"She doesn't really want to quit. She wanted me to know that she's worried about you. She says you're like a bear with a toothache and your work is slipping."

"It's this thing with Jill. I thought we had a fun, casual, mutually satisfying relationship going, and now I'm losing my mind because I can't see her. I don't understand it."

"I do. You're in love with that girl."

"What the hell good does that do me?"

"You really are in a bad mood, aren't you? You know I play tennis with Jill, and I can tell you that her mind hasn't been on her game lately. She wants to be with you too."

"Why is she such a stickler for the rules, then?"

"Because she's a good lawyer. Believe me, you don't want anything to do with the kind that cut corners when they want something."

"So what am I supposed to do now?"

"Short term, get it together and stop feeling sorry for yourself. You know this will end as soon as Jill finishes her trial. Long term, I've already told you what to do. Meanwhile, go give your secretary an apology and a couple days off with pay. She's better to you than you deserve."

"Like you?"

"Exactly."

So I did, and tossed in a day at the local day spa at my expense. I knew I couldn't afford to lose her. Then I buckled down and channeled my frustration into hard work until the trial rolled around.

There really were at least five sides to the landslide trial, and a whole herd of lawyers in the courtroom to match. They called me on the last day of the trial, and I testified to my opinion and then defended it to all the other lawyers who cross examined me. Jill did it with a perfectly straight face and her usual excellent grasp of the facts. The last in line was a weaselly looking guy with a supercilious look on his face.

"Ms. Williams had a lot of questions for you, didn't she?"

"About the same as the rest of you, I'd say."

"Isn't it true that you're dating her?"

"Not at the moment."

He was smirking, and the other lawyers were looking slightly disgusted.

"But you were?"

"Yes."

"Why aren't you now?"

"She refuses to talk to someone else's expert outside of court before trial."

"So you're hoping to start again when this trial is over?"

What could I say?

"Absolutely."

That got me a faint smile from Jill, which was the first hint she'd given that she knew me outside of court. The weasel didn't know when to stop.

"This was a sexual relationship?"

Jill turned beet red. The little weasel was lucky he was behind his table out of my reach. The senior lawyer in the bunch rose.

"Objection, relevance."

"Sustained."

"But, Your Honor..."

The judge, a gray haired veteran of a thousand courtroom battles, spoke coldly.

"There are some questions that no decent man will ask or answer. Sit down."

He turned to Jill.

"Ms. Williams, unlike some in this room, you've done a fine job of presenting your case thoroughly and professionally. You're an outstanding attorney. I'm not blind to the fact that you're also a very attractive young woman. If you didn't have a romantic life I would wonder what's wrong with young men these days. That's nothing for you to be embarrassed about. I don't see that it has anything to do with this case and I don't want to hear any more about it."

I heard a familiar voice as I reached the landing halfway down the courthouse steps at the end of the day.

"Ben, wait up!"

Jill came flying down the steps behind me, and I caught her as she started to stumble, spinning her around a couple times. Her arms went around my neck.

"So you still want to pick up where we left off?"

I grinned back at her.

"Absolutely."

The weasel's high pitched voice interrupted the kiss.

"I knew it!"

I carefully set Jill aside and turned.

"I knew you two were still dating! I'm telling the judge about this!"

All the pent up frustration of the last several weeks was behind the left hook to his solar plexus. I have to admit that it felt good. He stopped gloating and staggered around bent over and gasping for air.

"Assault! You assaulted me!"

He looked up at the other lawyers from the trial coming down the steps in a group.

"You all witnessed this! He's going to jail!"

The senior guy- the same one who broke up the personal questions about Jill- spoke first.

"It looked to me like you tripped going down the stairs and he saved your neck. That's more than I would have done if you had tried to embarrass my wife."

The rest of them nodded in agreement.

"You've humiliated yourself enough for one day, young man. Go home."

The weasel looked at the hard, unfriendly stares of the rest of the group, hung his head, and went down the stairs without another word. The spokesman turned to Jill.

"Ms. Williams, I agree with the judge. You're an excellent lawyer and there's nothing wrong with having a personal life. I suspect that Mr. McLoughlin's opinion on whether you're attractive is the only one that matters, so I have no comment on that. If you ever get tired of working for the State, call me. My firm will double your current salary." Jill beamed. He turned to me.

"Mr. McLoughlin, you did an excellent job as well. I'll call you the next time I need an engineer."

"As long as the State's not involved. I learned my lesson this time. These enforced separations are no fun at all."

"Well, I can tell you what I did when I caught the prettiest girl in town looking at me the way Ms. Williams looks at you. That was thirty five years, three kids, and a bunch of grandkids ago. You need to sort this out for yourselves, though."

He put a hand on my shoulder and pulled me with him as he turned to go, speaking quietly.

"You've got quite a left hook, son. I would have done the same thing, but don't make a habit of it, OK?"

He slapped me on the back and walked off without waiting for a response. Jill shook her head and slid her hand into mine.

"My knight errant rides again. I should probably be mad at you for punching that creep over me, but somehow I'm not feeling it."

"He must be one of those ones you refused to go out with."

"How did you know?"

"Recognized the type. What a loser. Anyway, can I take you to dinner?"

"I need to go unload all my trial materials at the office. How about I bring dinner to your place when I'm done?"

"Sure. Pack a bag and bring a nice dress or two. We're going away for the weekend."

"Where?"

"It's a surprise."

Jill couldn't stop yawning over dinner, and wandered off toward the back of my house soon after. She was sound asleep in my bed when I went to look for her. I did my chores and eventually crawled in with her, and she curled up to me without waking up. The trial had really worn her out. I woke her up early the next morning. She smiled and kissed me.

"I almost forgot how much I like waking up with you. Last night wasn't what I had planned, though."

"Same here, but at least you're back where you belong."

She kissed me again, and things started warming up quick. I had to stop way too early.

"As much as I'd like to spend the morning in bed with you, we've got a plane to catch."

Her eyes widened.

"A plane? What are you up to?"

"Get dressed and you'll find out."

She quickly showered and dressed and I drove her down to the harbor.

"A float plane? Ben, what is this?"

"Hurry up and jump aboard."

We found our seats with a handful of other people in the plane. The pilot turned to speak instead of using a loudspeaker.

"Welcome to the regular Victoria shuttle. I'm your pilot..." and on through the standard safety lecture.

"Victoria? I've never been there."

"You're going to love it. Relax and enjoy the flight."

Victoria is the most beautiful city in what, in my opinion, is the most beautiful place in the world. It sits on the south tip of Vancouver Island just across the water from the northwest corner of the continental United States, and most of it hasn't changed much since about 1900. The plane landed on the harbor right in front of our destination.

"The Empress? My God, Ben, I've heard so much about this!"

The Empress Hotel is a gorgeous pile of brick that was built by the Canadian Pacific Railroad around 1908. It was a favorite of the British royal family back when Canada was part of the British Empire, and when you walk in you think you're back in the days of the Empire. The interior has been carefully maintained exactly as it was built.

"My mother used to tell me stories about afternoon tea here when I was a little girl!"

"We have reservations for tea this afternoon. Let's find our room, get unpacked, and figure out what to do next."

"Ben, are you crazy? What is this costing you?"

"What's the point of working hard if I can't spoil my girl once in a while? Don't worry about it."

We spent a good part of the day wandering around the formal English gardens that surrounded the harbor area before heading back for afternoon tea. In my totally unbiased opinion, Jill was by far the most beautiful girl in the room in her flowery summer dress. From the looks she kept getting, most of the men in the room thought the same. Toward the end of tea, I reached for her hand.

"Jill, I really hated being separated from you these last few weeks. The only positive part is that it made me realize how much I love you, and that I never want to be separated from you again. I need to do something I should have done long ago."

I pulled a small box out of the pocket of my suit jacket.

"Jill, I want us to be together forever. Will you marry me?"

She didn't hesitate.

"Yes! Yes! Yes!"

I somehow got the ring on her finger with trembling hands, and a bottle of champagne appeared from nowhere.

Late that night, in our room, Jill was studying her left hand as it rested on my bare chest. She had hardly been able to keep her eyes off it during the brief periods we weren't otherwise occupied.

"Where did you find such a lovely ring?"

"I had Kim pick it out. She's been pushing me to do this for a long time. If you don't like it, though, we can exchange it for something else."

"I can't imagine loving anything more. Except you, of course."

A year later she wandered into my home office, holding an open file. She had her hair pulled back, reading glasses on and a pen behind her ear.

"Hey, Ben, what's an Atterberg limit?"

"Have we talked about my consulting fee?"

She walked over to my easy chair and put a hand on either arm, making sure I got a good look down my old button down shirt past her gently swinging breasts to the bright red silk thong that was the only other thing she had on.

"I'm sure I can think of something you'll like as soon as I finish this project."

"Sounds like an offer I can't refuse. Just don't forget."

She perched on the arm of my chair and ran her fingers through my hair, sending chills down my spine.

"Why do you think I'm absent minded?"

"You wouldn't be here if you hadn't left your cell phone in my truck the first time we met."

"Good Lord, I've married the village idiot! You still think that was an accident?"

"It wasn't?"

She kissed me, and I pulled her down into my lap.

"I was rescued by a brave, kind, handsome knight errant who wasn't trying to get my phone number. Sometimes a damsel in distress has to be her own fairy godmother."

"I sure wanted to see you again, but it seemed like a dirty trick to hit on you under the circumstances."

"I probably would have blown you off if you had. The fact that you were too decent to try made me decide to give you a reason to call me."

"You've been one step ahead of me this whole time, haven't you?"

"I still am, big guy, and don't you forget it."

She curled up in my lap, flipped her file open, and settled her glasses in place.

"Now help me finish this stupid project so I can remind you why I'm worth it."

And she is.